SHANE SHORTS

SHAHIN RIAZ

Made with ♥ on the Notion Press Platform
www.notionpress.com

To God. My Parents. My family

Contents

Acknowledgements

No more acknowledgements in life !!!

1

The AI BUG

Shane glanced over to his laptop which read 12 June 2075, lost in thought, not knowing what he was doing with his life or at work. "Happy Birthday to me" GROANNN. At 40, working at a mid-management level of a technology giant, he had been going through a rut for quite some time now and exploring other options to move away from his saturated work life. A loving wife and two sweet little kids were his only salvaging points to get through stressful or boring days at work, but even that was turning out to be a struggle with late baby wail nights catching up with his age. The monotonous routine craved for some excitement.

It was one such boring work-day when Shane decided to explore his usual quota of LinkedIn job opportunities when 3 things happened simultaneously.

A ping!!! A buzz!!! A shriek!!!

Ping - A notification on LinkedIn from an anonymous profile "Don't want to be the code? BE THE BUG! Meet me"

Buzz - A bug buzzed past Shane's laptop.

Shriek - "Shane!!! Why haven't you deployed the code to fix the bug? shrieked his boss".

A range of emotions swept through Shane. Rage at his boss, curiosity at seeing a bug inside the clean environment of their office and bewilderment at the BUG message on his LinkedIn chat box. He quickly minimized his screen and after whimpering out an apologetic response to his boss quickly went over to restroom. He opened his LinkedIn account on his mobile and quickly scanned the contents of the message. The message was generic and asked him to meet the sender at a café that night. Although confused, why the three-phenomenon happened at the same time, a renewed sense of hope was instilled in Shane's mind. Out of curiosity he decided to visit the café that night.

Shane walked into the café 15 mins before the appointment time mentioned in the message and took a corner seat oblivious to the busy world. He was jittery and explored every customer of the café with a suspicious eye. A gentleman walked into the café and slipped into the seat next to Shane. He looked classy and wore expensive clothing. "Hello and thanks for accepting the invite" he said as he extended his hands towards Shane. Shane shook his hands and asked uneasily "Who are you and why did you message me on LinkedIn". The stranger chuckled and replied, "It wasn't me who had pinged, it was one of the many like me". "What do you mean" Shane was confused as hell. "You are now talking to an AI engineered humanoid who has very little interest for human beings like you. However, you possess a specific set of skills which would help us overpower the human race and enslave them". "What the hell are you talking about? and why would I help you enslave human beings like me?" Shane was at his wits end. "Humans are bugs and not suited to running a clean environment. Just like how you eliminate bugs at home and also how you would remove one from your code to run a smooth application (chuckle), our job is to cleanse this world of the bugs called humans. You get a chance to upgrade yourself to be a humanoid in the process, that's our negotiating factor in this bargain and if you don't get to do it, we find someone else".

"But what happens to my family, my wife, kids parents?" Shane was desperate now

"You don't need a wife or kids or parents once you are a humanoid, you will be one for yourself and get to enjoy all emotions without a heart.Here, take this device with you and contemplate the rights and wrongs in your life, if you feel the right thing is to join us activate the device and we will come looking for you". The humanoid left as quickly as it had arrived.

Shane was shaking again with mixed emotions of excitement, rage, and bafflement. WHAT THE HELL HAD JUST HAPPENED!!! He stumbled out of his booth and rushed home shaking. He was still mumbling gibberish after arriving home and his wife had to pacify him for 2 hours before a semblance of sanity returned. He lay in bed deep in thought figuring out the events of the day. He was almost dozing off after reassuring himself that it was just a bad day dream when 3 things happened simultaneously.

A ping!!! A buzz!!! A shriek !!!

Ping - A notification on his device "It's not a dream, last chance, BE THE BUG!!!"

Buzz - The "same" bug buzzed past his eyes

Shriek - "Daddy Daddy, a bug!!!"

That was Shane's night done. Tossing and turning in sleep. Contemplating what was happening with his life. Whether these were signs of nature giving it back to him for his troubled past and present with a better future. His wife was constantly cursing him as all the tossing and turning was disturbing the kids as well. Later when his wife and kids were asleep, Shane wept uncontrollably just looking at them imagining if this would be one of the last nights, he would be seeing them and resort to living a lonely life.

Next day, Shane was back in the office disheveled, dark black bags under his eyes. "Were you up all night watching porn?" snorted out his manager. Shane didn't even bother glancing in the direction of his boss and walked right up to his desk. His boss took this as a sign of insubordination and started yelling at him about some late deployments which had created escalations for him. Shane was tired and lost in his own thoughts and was not in the mood to retort back. After a while of blasphemous shouting the boss went back to his cabin shaking his head. The other employees were all looking at Shane now, some with empathy, while the others enjoying the show. Shane closed his laptop and went out for some air. He kept replaying the previous day's events in his mind and was trying to feel sorry for himself. As he was about to step back with a resigned sense of hopelessness, three things happened simultaneously,

A ping!!! A buzz!!! A shriek!!!

Ping - "Don't give up on yourself yet, your replacement is nearly found, don't waste your time here, BE THE BUG!!!"

Buzz - "Am I imagining now" the bug buzzzzed by Shane.

Shriek - Shrieks followed a thud, 2 Volkswagen beetles had crashed into each other nearly killing the inmates of the car.

The signs were too strong to ignore for Shane now. His wife's chide from the previous night and the constant snide from his boss had worked up an inconsolable anguish and pain in him. All the years of loathe and self-doubt came right back to him. Was this going to be his escape mechanism. Shane activated the device.

"What do you want me to do?" Shane responded back to the humanoid. "Same place, same time, be there" the response was instant.

Shane waited anxiously and made sure he had chosen the same spot as last time.

"So, you came finally" It was a different gentle-oid this time.

"Who are you" Shane asked, "Oh just one of the many who think alike and soon you will too as well" the new humanoid chimed in.

"All of you look the same, smart, good looking, almost too perfect to be true" Shane.

"Oh, we are perfect in most ways than you can really think of" humanoid chuckled.

"Let's get down to business. Almost 95% of the world population use smartphones, the rest of the 5% we will deal with later. As you know your world folks are so intent on providing us with data with your stupid reels, eagerness to show the world what they are doing on a daily basis even if this means they need to share their bedroom secrets, their bathroom routine, what they eat, where they shit, our super intelligent systems have almost all of the information required to enslave them, so in short their IQ is locked in with us." "What we are lacking" continued the humanoid "is the EQ factor. We would like to go one over the IQ element and marry the EQ element of humans to it. Once we have this, we will make humans fall in love with their smartphone and vice versa. We will get them to a state where we force humans to destroy one another for either love or money."

"Now this is where you come in, with your knowledge of big data mapping we want you to figure out a logic to connect the IQ information we have with some EQ models that we have built up based on hear hear more data that we have".

"This is easier said than done" Shane was getting defensive already "You are talking about mapping gazillions of actual defined data with a million data models".

"Good, you just said it will be difficult and not impossible. This was the reason why we had to dispose of the last guy. He completely trashed the idea, and we didn't take kindly to it".

"What do you mean by disposed of him?"

"Well, let's leave it at that since you have agreed to work on it. You have a month's time to come up with a solution and since you are privy to our little secret there is no backing out now".

"A month will not be enough" said Shane not believing what he was actually bargaining about.

"A month is what you will get" replied the humanoid coolly. "Any other question?"

"Yes, why me? Why did you choose me? I am not even the most experienced person in my organization".

"That you may not be, but you are the most vulnerable person at the moment and that is what works for us" the humanoid was clearly enjoying the pain being inflicted on Shane at this point.

The humanoid disappeared in a jiffy leaving Shane stumped.

Shane left the café and revved up his engine towards home. He was not sure why he had agreed to be part of this plan in the first place. A humanoid taking advantage of his frailties and making him think of abandoning his family. He had to get himself and his family out of the town and as far away from town as possible. He had decided to move back to his village and called up his wife to pack up immediately without explaining to his confused wife. Just as he was about to turn around the corner of his house, three things happened simultaneously,

A ping!!! A buzz!!! A shriek!!!

Ping - "Leaving the town will not solve your problems, leaving the world would. I AM COMING FOR YOU. RIP QUASHED BUG"

Buzz – "Get off my head" Shane said to the imaginary bug in his head.

Shriek - "Bug off asshole" Shane almost killed an old lady by crashing into her.

Shane couldn't wait any more and stopped the car midway on the road and started running home, he could see the world collapsing in front of his eyes as he ran towards his home and his wife who was waiting for him at the doorstep with open arms. Shane was shouting and crying his wife's name as he ran towards her and suddenly "THWACK"... "Wake up Shane. WAKE UP!!! What the hell are you shouting about, it's just a nightmare. The kids are asleep, DO NOT WAKE THEM UP". Shane shot up drenched in sweat and picked up his mobile. The wallpaper, which was a detailed photo of a bug he had captured read 2AM 12th June 2023. His sleepy wife was miffed with his antics and would have killed him had it not been a nightmare. "We are alive, we are alive" "I love you, I love you" Shane started hugging his wife and kids one after the other. "Get off me you fool and leave my kids alone. Go to sleep, you and your crazy dreams". Shane was beaming and laid down thinking what the hell was the dream all about. He was just about to doze off again when THREE BLOODY THINGS HAPPENED AGAIN SIMULATANEOUSLY,

A PING!!! A BUZZ!!! A SHRIEK!!!

2

The Pseudo HIM

Was he real, fake, or a real fake? Is this really happening? Thoughts came flooding back to Shane as he reflected on the events of the night.

Shane was getting back from a late-night party. It was a dark and wet night, and Shane had had quite a few to drink. The rain was pelting down in sheets, turning the curvy road into a mirror of black water. The car's windscreen was losing its battle against the rain. Shane was nearly driving blind when he felt a thud on his vehicle. He had to slam his brakes to stop his car. He got out to check if whatever he hit was ok. Nothing was in sight for miles.

"Get a grip, Shane," she muttered to herself. "You're just tired."

He had presumed it was a passing stray animal or a tree trunk on the road and carried on. As he pulled away from the spot and glanced into the rear-view mirror, he noticed a familiar face clenching his stomach and stopped immediately. He got out of the car and looked behind, but there wasn't anyone in the vicinity. Things were getting creepy; he had gotten back into the car and sped back home. He blamed the illusion on alcohol and went to sleep.

The next day Shane was up as usual and off to work. He was the product head of a MNC eCommerce giant and bored sick of his job. The only problem was that all of his other interests in life had vanquished with age and left him stuck in the dull eComm world he was in now. As Shane sipped through his morning coffee at the office diner, a news reporter was blurting out a missing person case on TV. Something caught his eye.

"Inspector Anbu has been missing since last night. He was on the hunt for international arms dealer Alexander."

Shane's jaw dropped, and his mind raced back to the previous night. He had felt the familiarity in the face he saw in the rearview mirror yesterday. The greying version of Inspector Anbu brought back memories of 17 years ago. Inspector Anbu had sought Shane and his gang's help to solve a murder mystery in their college. The initial interactions between them were hostile, to say the least, but eventually both had to join forces to find the identity of the real killer.

Shane thought of reactivating his old boy's gang WhatsApp group and then thought the better of it. Although the gang was now dormant and restricted to happy birthday messages on WhatsApp, he knew that once he would discuss these kinds of details, one of the blabbermouths in the group would talk about it.

Shane felt a sudden thrill inside. He wondered if he could resolve the case by himself. But first, he had to ascertain that what he saw the previous night wasn't an illusion. Also, the stakes were higher this time around. As opposed to a principal killing a peon, he would be dealing with an international arms dealer if the news was right. Shane shuddered at the very thought. He decided to give it a shot anyway, as it was the only exciting thing in his empty life now.

Shane had to find answers, and some of them fast. He went back to the same stretch of road with a few tools (just in case). The road itself was trodden on by tire marks and footsteps a plenty. Shane looked around the bushes from the spot where he remembered he had stopped the car the previous night. Nothing out of the ordinary, again plenty of footsteps. He walked a little further and discovered another path that had two sets of foot marks. He followed the footmarks and came to a halt in front of a run-down abandoned building. Shane was in two minds to explore further when he heard a snap some distance ahead. Shane's heart skipped and beat. He found a bush to hide and watched.

He saw a man walk towards the building. He was carrying a huge sack that had blood stains on it. Shane figured the worst. He couldn't get closer to the building without risking being seen. So he waited. The man (presumably Alexander) started chopping up something in the building. Shane's stomach started growling out of sheer disgust. He couldn't shore up enough courage to look, though. After about half an hour, the stranger left the building with the same sack in hand, this time blood dripping from the sack. Shane felt sick in his stomach and wanted to belch but kept it to himself. He waited for the man to leave and then went inside the building.

The building was completely isolated and resembled a rathole. Leftover food was strewn across the floor. The place stank of alcohol, with cig butts littering the floor. It looked like the place had been used by more than one person recently. Shane made sure to not touch anything with his hands. Shane found some photographs on the table. On closer investigation, he found that they were mugshots of Inspector Anbu. Shane's worst fears were being confirmed, and he didn't like it one bit. Shane popped up his mobile to find Alexander's photo online. The photographs were of a younger Alexander and looked sketchy. Shane couldn't say for a fact if the man who had walked into the building was Alexander. Shane looked through the rest of the items available in the building—the knife used to cut through the meat, a chainsaw, and some old clothes.

Shane's first instinct was to rush to a police station and report the incident, but something held him back. Something was not right. Although the strange man resembled Alexander's build, Shane wasn't sure for a fact if this was Alexander. Also, it would be difficult to explain to the cops how he had found the abandoned building. Shane decided to dig further to learn more about Alexander and Inspector Anbu.

Inspector Anbu, after the famous College Collude expedition (as was the case called), had risen up the ranks pretty quickly. Quite recently he was promoted to Special Squad assigned with cases related to the national security of the country. The squad was given a free hand to deal with the cases as they deemed fit and reported directly to the Prime Minister's office. Anbu and his team had carried out four special operations to thwart arms and terrorist activities. Just this last operation had proven to be a more difficult assignment, and he was hell bent on tacking down Alexander.

Getting details on Alexander was proving to be more difficult. Shane visited the public library and tried to dig up the past of Alexander. Alexander or Alex had a troubled childhood and had run away from home as a kid. The next time Alex's name resurfaced back as a dreaded don dealing with arms mainly. No details of the time in between were available. All the photos on Alexander were not fully clear either. Alexander had a bounty on his head due to his latest escapades and suspected links with terrorists.

The cat and mouse between Anbu and Alexander had been going on for the past 6 months, with Alexander narrowly escaping from Anbu's clutches a couple of times. Some articles had pointed out that Anbu was under tremendous pressure to nail down Alexander before the Chinese Premier's visit to the country and time was running out. Some reports even indicated that Alexander had fled the country and was operating from elsewhere. The most recent news snippets indicated Anbu was tracking down Alexander's sudden visit to India and being in hot pursuit.

Every bit of news suggested a cruel end to Anbu's dedication to eradicating crime from the country. Shane felt a sense of despair at nearly knowing everything and yet not being able to do anything. Shane felt he needed to go back to the building again and try to ambush whoever was the strange man. It was a risk, and he had to take it. Shane decided to confide in his most trusted friends, Peter and Mandy. Peter and Mandy were trained in advanced martial arts and could help if required with an ambush. He quickly assembled the boys, who were flabbergasted with his request, but decided to go through with the plan anyway for the sheer excitement. The plan was simple and yet stupid considering a lot of parameters were not taken into consideration. For instance, what if the man was not alone? Was it really Anbu cut up in the bag? Would the man return at all? There were more questions than answers. Also, the real question was: if they were really dealing with Alexander the dreaded don, why was he alone? Would their martial arts (although advanced) be enough?

Shane, Peter, and Mandy waited for the sun to set and made their way to the abandoned building. They decided to take the alternate route to the place. It was yet another chilly rainy night with the rain pelting down. It was extremely difficult to figure out the way, especially with no torchlight or natural light to guide them. On reaching the building, Shane could see a glint of light coming out of the room. Shane peered into the room and found the strange man he had seen the other day gorging on some pizza and yelling at the same time. He was now accompanied by an accomplice.

At first glance, he looked to be a fine young athlete from behind. His figure was tall, his posture unnaturally still, like he had been looking into distant nothing for a long time. He wore a long, dark coat, which covered his neck and brushed the ground as he shifted ever so slightly. The coat was buttoned all the way up to his neck, hiding any glimpse of meanness beneath.

As he turned, his face—what little Shane could see of it—was gaunt and angular and very familiar. He was clean-shaven. His cheekbones were sharp, and the hollows beneath his eyes deepened by the dim light. But it was his eyes that unsettled him the most. He had seen them before. They were dark and cold. They were cold and calculating, as if he could see through his enemies and if a request passed them.

His hair was slicked back, black and streaked with silver, though uneven, as if he had cut it by himself in a hurry or didn't care for appearances. There was a tension in his face, though—like a coiled spring, ready to act at any moment.

To his horror, Shane realized that he was looking at the very own Inspector Anbu!!!
The air around him felt colder than before, like he carried with him the weight of the country. He didn't speak, but the silence between them was thick with unspoken words. The room seemed to shrink; every instinct told Shahin to leave, and yet he stayed. Anbu turned around and spoke to the stranger under his breath. The stranger snorted as he gorged on his meal. Anbu was half disgusted with the stranger's manners and continued to talk to him, and the stranger nodded once in a while.
What was happening here? Who was this guy with Anbu? Where is Alexander?

THUD !!!

Peter had tripped on a shovel next to him. The trio was exposed. Anbu quickly whipped out a gun from his waistcoat and pointed it at Shane. Realization hit him suddenly.

"Well, well, well, who do we have here? If it is not the MRPSC boys, the gang of no gooders. Shane right? ... and... Pee, Peter, and Mandy? Where are the rest of the gang? Must be whileing away their life in some foreign country." Although Anbu's voice was the same as before, there was a new evil sneer to it now. "But why? and how? and who is this guy?"

"Wait, wait," chuckled Anbu. "One at a time. First, the easy answer: He clenched his stomach, as if in pain. "No, this isn't Alex as you would have imagined. Knowing you, you would have done your research, although I am not sure what your motive is behind this."

"I discovered this building by chance after the escapade the day before yesterday. Am sure you remember seeing me the other night?"

"Oh, it was you. I see. I had noted down the number and decided to take care of the owner after all this was over."

"And to think that my only motive was to make sure you were okay or make sure to get you justice in case you were..."

"Dead?" Anbu was enjoying this conversation. "Ok, now since that mystery is settled. This is Adam, Alex's twin brother. Unlike Alex, he is more interested in food and some naughty action." Adam smiled sheepishly.

"... and why? Well, why not? Dammit, why NOT?????"

"17 years ago, when I was your age back then and fresh out of the College Collude case, I was expecting great things in life." "The next thing I knew, I was transferred to the wilderness of nowhere."

"That's why I didn't find you when I came to call you for our department symposium," Shane muttered under his breath.

"What?" Anbu continued "Never mind. So, as I was saying, I was crestfallen, to say the least. I had given my all up until then and lost my wife to the force, and yet for solving such a high-profile case, all I got was a transfer. I got to know later that your principal, with all his political connections, was living a king's life in prison, and instead of getting me killed, he wanted me to suffer. I had to make a choice: face the wrath of the devil or side with the devil and so on." Just as Anbu was about to finish, an old man with a cane walked into the building.

Shane gasped. It was his college principal!!! The College Collude was happening all over again!!!

"Who are these brats?" The principal was in a gross mood.
"You don't even recognize your old students?" grinned Anbu. "These are the guys who helped me put you away 17 years ago."
"Aaagh, those idiot Gang of No Gooders, huh. They were trouble then and still are." Princi barked at the guys. "If it were not for my son, I would have made your lives miserable as well. Anyway, better late than never."
"Wait, wait, I am yet to complete my story, and then we can dispose of these guys. I decided to meet your principal to see if there was a way out of this misery. He then confided in me to take care of his arms business along with Alex and Adam till he was in prison. I decided to live a double life: savior by day, villain by night. Everything was going well. Alex, who was a wanted criminal, managed our business abroad, and me and Adam made sure there was constant supply in and out to help Alex. This was when Alex decided to come back and make things difficult. In the meantime, I got deputed to this special squad. I tried to put sense into Alex, but he wouldn't budge. He suspected me and Adam were making a bigger cut here. Well, the boss ordered us to finish off Alex. Alex smelt foul and threatened to expose me. He had been tailing me since the last 3 days and studying my routine, hence these beautiful pics." Anbu held up the

pics that Shane had seen the previous day. "Well, Alex didn't take into consideration the fact that I was a cop and bloody good one. With Adam's help I traced Alex to this old shack. I had no option but to kill him. This was the piece of action you would have seen the other night," Shane smirked after clenching his stomach. "Adam, an expert at demolishing things, made sure he tore his brother into shreds and fed them to the dogs thereby getting rid of any proof against us. I just didn't want to take the risk of being a National hero by declaring that I had killed lex as I didn't want the other cops coming behind me with the investigation. And now, we will end all of this so we can go back to our peaceful pseudo lives."

"Kill those rascals," bellowed the principal.

"Yes sir. Hands up and kneel, you 3. Giving you a taste of your college days."

Shane slowly pulled out his hands from his pockets and raised them with a mobile phone in his hands. "Anbu, although I came looking for your murderer or at least a way to help you out of this, and I used the very same crap technique you had used 17 years ago on the criminal standing next to you. The year we helped put this menace away in prison, I had come to your office to invite you to our department symposium as a chief guest. There I had met with Inspector Cheran, who had taken your place, and to this date I have a great friendship with that nobleman. He and his force are waiting outside for you, and yeah, you can't spin another web of tales as he has listened to your entire story already." Shane motioned to the phone in his hand, which was already on a call.

"Well, I guess I have nothing to lose then, so be it." Anbu shot the principal and Adam in one go.
Crash!!! Thud!!!

Anbu had his pistol in the direction of the boys and had fired a shot. As they drove for cover, Inspector Cheran and his team had smashed the door open and surrounded Inspector Anbu. Shane, Mandy, and Peter had escaped the spray of bullets by a whisker.

"The police force will never expose me. I will die a warrior, as the man who died in operation of killing three dreaded international criminals." With these words, as Anbu was preparing to pull the trigger, Inspector Cheran got a bullseye shot on Anbu's hand, and Anbu dropped the gun as the shot hit his arm.
"Not so fast, Anbu. I used to respect you immensely. You have let yourself and the entire police force down. I will make sure you will rot in prison forever." Inspector Cheran took Anbu away.

"I GUESS WE WILL MEET AGAIN." Anbu sent a striking warning to Shane with the chilling message!!!

This Is Just A Start To Shane Stories...